GHOSTS AVENUE

USA Today Bestselling Author

TAYA RUNE

Purple
Realm
PUBLISHING

Taya's Steamy Books

<u>Steamy Contemporary</u>

Champagne Resolutions

War of Hearts

<u>Bewitching Twisted Fairytales</u>

The Charming Thief

<u>Fantasy Romance</u>

The Right To Rule Series

Outcast

Lethal

Fatal

Betrayal

Denial

Loyal (Coming Soon)

<u>Paranormal Mystery Romance</u>

<u>*Enchanted Underworld*</u>

Weapons of the Fae Queen Series
The Warlock's Lair
The Oracle's Court
The Nymph's Realm
The Dragon's Garden
Gates of Ascension Series
Ghosts Avenue
Elven Ingress

Check out her website for all her current works.
tayarune.com

Content Warning

If you are concerned about content, please check Taya's website for a list of warnings for all of her books.
It can be found under the 'Books' tab.

tayarune.com

For those standing at the edge of truth—
may you choose what heals.

Chapter 1
Katya

"Go straight in." The guard to her left opened the door, while the other nodded and moved aside, allowing her to enter the private sitting room of the Fae Queen, and ultimate ruler of the Enchanted Underworld, Queen Stellamaris.

Katya inclined her head and stepped into the room to find the Fae Queen, General Owen, and Weapons Master Kirkpatrick, all sitting at a small round table in the far corner of the room. They were pouring over a map, as far as Kat could make out.

"Come, sit," beckoned Kirkpatrick.

"Yes, Sir." Kat walked quickly to the indicated chair and curtsied to the queen before sitting. She remained silent and waited for someone to address her further. It was rare that Kat felt intimidated by anyone, but these three were the true leaders of the Enchanted Underworld, no matter how much the other Kings and Queens felt, and she was sitting at a table with them.

"Have you given much thought to how you would use your team in this current situation?" General Owen raised his head from looking at the map and watched her with eyes the same color blue as his daughter's, Princess and Weapon of the Fae Queen, Jazlynn.

"I would never presume," she began, but an almost imperceptible scowl from Kirkpatrick made her change her words. "Yes, I have."

"Go on, speak freely," urged Owen.

Kat relaxed her shoulders and looked at the map of Earth. It was marked with all the countries of the Human Plane, but there was an overlay of almost clear vellum that had different markings and sigils. It was easier to stare at the map than look at anyone in particular as she spoke her next words. "I would send each of the squad to the locations of each of the gates to check that there are no armies amassing on one of the Planes." Katya continued to study the map and added, "Once we know their locations."

"We know some of their locations already," commented Kirkpatrick.

"I would have an easier job of assigning the squad if I knew each location," Katya said.

"That's why we didn't move that map when you came in," he replied. "Here and here are two of the gates." Kirkpatrick pointed to two shapes on the vellum.

Katya stood and looked at the detailed map. She quickly realized that the map of the Earth under the vellum was colored by continents, with the overlay representing the planes and which continent it was linked to. The pictures that the Weapons Master had indicated were hexagon in shape, black in color, and had a small drawing in white. Kat leaned forward to get a better look at the drawings. She looked up in shock and then back down. The drawings were the smaller versions of the pictures she had seen on the wall when she had been trapped at the Oracle's Court.

She studied the first picture. It was a set of double doors that arched and ended with a point at the top. From the tip of the door and down each side were dots, but Katya knew from seeing a larger etching that they were circles with the same four symbols in them, repeating in the same order. Flower, sun, leaf, moon. The symbol of what she now understood was the gate to the Elven Plane indicated that it was in Northern America.

It made little sense for Chaos to try to reach the Bridge to Heaven from the Elven Ingress, as he wouldn't get far. The wrath of the mighty war machine, which was America, if an army of demons appeared near their fake Area 51, would be swift if he dared to approach from there. Katya shook her head, wondering if her friend, Scarlett, knew that not only did she guard the most extensive magical library on the seven planes, but she also kept watch over the portal that led to the long abandoned fourth plane, the Elven Empire.

Katya switched her focus to the symbol he had pointed at. "And where does this gate lead to?" she asked without lifting her head.

"Plane six. It is the Ghosts Avenue," General Owen, Jazlynn's father, answered. "Each of the Planes have a Ghosts Avenue, though they name them differently."

The symbol in the hexagon had two pillars with a thin path leading between the two. Katya recalled that in the larger version there had been waves lapping at the pathway and each pillar had seven circles running vertically. She knew the top pillar, had a wrought iron like gate, and one had a tree, but couldn't remember the rest at the moment. Kat bent lower to study the vellum and the map underneath. She frowned as she attempted to understand what it meant.

"You say that each Plane has this gate? This is sitting on top of where we are." Kat looked up at the three. "And it doesn't show where the other gates are on the other planes."

Queen Stellamaris reached out and carefully lifted the vellum to reveal the map of Plane two, and there, directly underneath where the Enchanted Underworld symbol sat, was the one for the human plane. It was somewhere in China.

"It is called Tongtian Avenue. There are 999 steps to a cave opening that is translated as Heaven's Door." She gently laid the vellum back down. "Each Plane's Ghosts Avenue lays on top of the other in the four planes between heaven and hell."

Katya nodded. It made sense. "Okay, but where is it in this Plane?"

"It's the reason why the Crystal City was built here; to protect and keep watch over the gate. It is on the estates of the Royal family."

"Smart," commented Kat. "You can keep watch without anyone knowing. Easy to patrol the area and keep people away." She continued to study the map, taking note of many dots scattered throughout the Enchanted Underworld. About half of them had a cross over it. "These are the portals that lead to the other Planes?" She pointed at the one she had used to get to Chicago only a few days ago. "The ones with crosses are no longer stable?" she guessed.

She looked up to find three faces all with different but similar expressions on them. Weapons Master Kirkpatrick looked proud, General Owen impressed, and the Queen glowed with approval.

"My daughter will be lucky to have you when she takes the throne. You are smart, concise, and don't startle easily." Owen spoke frankly. "Yes, they are the portals between the Planes. As they falter and become unstable, we continue to have a small group of soldiers stationed at them to keep people from using them as there have been a few instances where people have been spliced in two when the portal malfunctioned."

"And we no longer have the knowledge to fix them? Or create new ones?" Katya spoke, but it was really a rhetorical question. It was frustrating, but Katya felt like there was something she was missing as she scanned the map for a clue that could help them find the other two gates. Knowing herself well enough to understand that the more she thought about it the more it wouldn't resolve itself, she had to let these things sit at the back of her mind and allow her thoughts to figure it out without forcing it.

"It seems with the return of Druids, there is much we only now understand we have lost to history. Perhaps once this crisis is over, Trell will have answers to our questions."

"Yes," Kat agreed. "And you could also ask the Keeper to search her extensive library. She's trustworthy enough to guard the Forgotten Ones and the complex that is Area 52, so I think she can be trusted to help with other matters." Katya looked at each of the leaders. "Or what is the point of having that huge magical library if not to use?"

No one answered Kat, but she didn't mind. She had spoken the truth and hoped they would see it that way, but now was not the time to push. Chaos's plan for revenge needed to be understood and dealt with first. Trell had given them some understanding of the renegade Druid's want for retribution as the Gods had punished the Angel Arella after she had fallen in love with Chaos and revealed secrets in the Angel's Scriptures and aided him in escaping his capture for centuries until they were both caught and judged on the Bridge.

"Is that all the information you have on these gates?" Kat asked.

"Yes," answered Kirkpatrick.

"Then returning to your original question of where I would put my team, I would have to admit that Jazlynn and Cael are a problem."

"How so?"

"Cael is valuable and powerful but absolutely not trustworthy."

"And Jazlynn is in love with him," Stellamaris finished.

"Well, yes." Kat looked over at the beautiful Fae Queen. "But I trust her to make the right choices when it comes to him."

"Good, so do I. Go on."

"I fear Jaz's days as a Weapon are numbered and we must limit her exposure at the moment. Named or not, she is your heir, and too many people know about it." Katya dared to look at each of the Fae. No one disagreed with her. "By using her mind speech abilities as a reason, she can stay on this Plane to help co-ordinate everyone. You can give her the task of checking on her own estate that the Ghosts Avenue gate is not compromised and also see if the two of them can figure out where the gate from Plane two to here is."

All three looked at her and Owen nodded to continue. "Send Calliope to check on the Elven Ingress at Area 52, and Twila and I will continue to investigate other leads until we are needed elsewhere."

"Good," Owen said. "Gather your team; we have a meeting in half an hour with the other rulers."

Chapter 2
Calliope

It was late afternoon, and Calliope had been feeling antsy all day. They had talked and talked and, in the end, gone around in circles trying to analyze Chaos' next move.

It felt good to be doing something, and she felt the edge of angst start to recede... though it was nowhere near gone.

A trickle of blood from her cut lip was the only indicator that he had landed a punch. She made no sound, no grunt of pain, nor exclamation of protest. She barely even rocked back on her feet.

"No wonder Artemis decided to drown you. I thought Chipmunk was jesting when he described your fight with her. She is a Dragon and you, a mere Fae."

"Mere Fae?" she muttered darkly. "Are you trying to piss me off more?" Calliope ducked as he swung wide with his huge fist and came up to punch him in the side, avoiding his kidneys, as she wasn't entirely certain her cousin, Katya, would be willing to heal them. But she hoped that punch hurt.

"I was just referring to how she would see you," Apollo protested mildly as he winced from the punch. "To her, you would be seen as no threat, which is why she insulted you by not providing you with a seat suited to your needs at the dinner table." He placed his hand on his chest. "I would never claim a Fae to be anything other than spectacular." Apollo abruptly jabbed sharp and hard, forcing Calliope to duck and weave to avoid the punch. "Without a Fae to heal my shoulder and wing after the blast at the Oracle's Court, I would never have been able to do that, or swim to the depths of the pool to save you," his voice had grown soft.

Calliope did not like to be reminded of almost drowning, and that was twice in the space of a few minutes. It was going to take some time to heal from that trauma, and she didn't really have time. She lashed out in frustration and kicked him on the chin, which was no easy feat considering he was seven foot tall, and she was only five foot five. Having wings to help propel her definitely helped in this case.

"Are you regretting your decision, yet?" she asked grumpily, deciding to change the subject from her near death.

"Which one would that be, sunshine?" He stepped back and rubbed his chin. "I have certainly made a few choices in the last twenty-four hours."

"The decision to abandon me and Chipmunk to babysit *her*." Calliope refused to say her name.

"Someone had to do it."

"Let her father do it."

"Her father is more than half the reason she is like she is." Apollo stepped back from what would have been another kick to his face. "Artemis has always deferred to me," he explained.

"That's because she wants to bed you," Calliope pointed out. She hated that she sounded jealous.

He arched a perfect eyebrow at her, as if to question her statement. Calliope refused to be drawn into it. She would rather bite her own tongue off than tell him that before Artemis had thrown Calliope into the pool, she had demanded to know what Calliope had that she didn't to make Apollo flirt with her. Artemis had revealed that he had never been like that with any of the Dragons at court. With a satisfying smack, Calliope landed a hit to his upper left arm.

"You really are amazingly strong," he admitted as he rubbed his arm.

Apollo pulled his black tunic off to inspect his arm and side. His torso was angular and well defined and brought back memories of her pressed against him.

"It's not going to work," she said and moved away to get a drink from the flask she had brought into the salle.

He raised his head from looking at his arm. "I don't know what you are talking about."

"Sure, you don't." Calliope barely stopped herself from stalking over to him and dragging his head down to hers to kiss him. Hard.

The door opened and Calliope was glad for the interruption. It halted her from doing something stupid. While last night had been hot and exactly what she needed to banish her dark memories, she had no intention of falling for Apollo or Julian. She was just peeved that Apollo had chosen to go back to the Dragon that had tried to murder her.

Katya stepped through the door, with Julian following closely behind her. "Oh, good, you are back. Did you find out anything new?" Calliope asked, ignoring the deliberate look of surprise on Kat's face as she took in the half naked, massive frame of the Wyvern, who was sporting several red marks where Calliope had hit him.

"You're bleeding," Kat pointed out helpfully.

"He got in a lucky punch," Calliope said, licking her lip carefully. It didn't feel too bad.

"Apollo, what the actual fuck?" exclaimed Julian. He stepped around Kat and moved to Calliope where, without asking, he lifted her chin and softly ran his thumb across her bleeding lip. "Sunshine, are you alright?"

Calliope panicked and pulled her chin away, stepping back abruptly. "I'm fine." She glared up at him, her eyes darting toward Kat.

Julian belatedly dropped his hand.

"Sunshine?" asked Kat, her voice neutral, but Calliope could sense the mirth underneath.

She turned to look at her cousin. "Where's your oracle?" Calliope asked, hoping to change the subject.

It was Kat's turn to look uncomfortable. She shrugged her shoulders. "How would I know?"

"Well, didn't you just come from his estate? Did he come back with you or not?" Calliope raised an eyebrow at Kat, deliberately trying to goad her cousin into responding and taking the conversation well away from the two men in the room arguing over her wellbeing.

"I have been back for a while and have had a private meeting with our bosses."

Calliope noted that Kat did not name who those bosses were, which in fairness, was correct procedure. Too many people knew they were Weapons; there was no point in revealing any more information, particularly in front of the Wyvern, Apollo. Calliope wanted to believe that he was one of the good guys, but his willingness to return to Artemis gave her pause.

Kat went on. "You." She pointed at Calliope. "Have been summoned to a meeting. Lord Apollo, you are to return to the Dragon Garden." She then jutted her chin toward Julian. "And you are to report to Trell, to learn more about being a Druid."

No one moved for several seconds which made Kat roll her eyes before she smirked at Calliope. "I'll give you boys some space to say goodbye to sunshine here." And with that parting shot, Kat spun on her heel and headed out the door, closing it firmly behind her.

Calliope glowered at her back but didn't retort. It would just make the teasing worse. Instead, she walked over to her small pile of belongings and began to dab at her lip with a towel that she wet with water from her drink bottle. She moved over to the mirrored wall and took a closer look. It was going to swell a little, but it wouldn't be too bad. In some bizarre way, she was secretly pleased that she would carry something with her for a short amount of time that would remind her of Teddy Bear. *Angel of mercy, you are a strange one sometimes,* Calliope told herself as she shook her head and turned away from the mirror. She almost turned back rather than face the two men standing in front of her, both with their arms crossed glaring at each other.

"What's your problem?" she asked, hoping to break the tension. "It better not be about me."

This made them both turn to face her. "I'm not the one with the problem," Lord Apollo rumbled, his voice so deep Calliope was surprised it didn't cause the floor to vibrate. "Chipmunk here is annoyed that I made you bleed." The Wyvern gave Julian a sidelong glance as if to challenge him.

"You're still recovering from—" Julian stopped when he saw the look Calliope threw him.

A small cough entered Calliope's mind, and she knew that Jazlynn was about to say something tele-pathically.

"What's taking so long? We are only waiting on you and the Nymph Queen."

"On my way."

The presence of Jaz left her mind and Calliope looked at both the hot men standing before her. "I don't have time for this. I've got a meeting to get to, as do both of you. It was a fun distraction and what I needed." She shrugged casually. "Thanks for a great night, but I've got work to do. Good luck with everything." And before either of them could do more than call her name, she was out the door and running up the path back to the palace.

Chapter 3
Katya

Nymph Queen Nemea cleared her throat, causing everyone to stop and look at her. "It would seem to me that I am the only one able to keep my key safe, so I should continue to hold it, wouldn't you say?" She looked around the room.

"I think taking it from its resting place without telling anyone and then not coming forward immediately when we thought it stolen is a large indicator that you are not to be fully trusted," rumbled Erebus, King of the Dragons and Wyverns.

"Are you really going to harp on that?" she asked wearily. "Can't we let bygones be bygones?"

"It needs to be in the safest place we can think of, and I don't think that's the Nymph and Vila Realm," Erebus said stubbornly.

"Well, I don't think the safest place is the Dragon Garden either. It turns out your daughter has a few anger issues that need to be sorted." Nemea threw a look at Calliope, but didn't say her name.

"What are you implying?" His voice grew deeper, and he leaned forward in his chair.

"I am not implying anything; I am saying it outright. Put a leash on that girl or we will not endorse her to become your heir."

Erebus glowered at her but said nothing further. *How could he?* Katya thought. *Nemea is not wrong.* Though it also occurred to Kat she had been told that Erebus had been quick to apologize for his daughter's behavior when they had been in private. Perhaps he blustered and growled because he thought he had to?

"Queen Stellamaris, where do you suggest we hide it?" interrupted Baron Martel, forever the diplomat. He sat next to the white-clothed fairy, Twila, who Katya noted unconsciously played with the large engagement ring on her hand. It turned out he had had it in his possession for several years, waiting for Twila to be ready to marry him, in the middle of last night he had finally popped the question.

The Fae Queen spoke. "It pains me to say, but I am unsure. It would not be prudent for us to put it back in a place it has been already," she began. "They are places he is familiar with. Putting it in Area 52 might seem wise on the surface, but do we want two things he seeks in the same place? I believe Scarlett should continue to protect the Keeper's Tome; she has proven she is capable."

"I am sorry to interrupt, but would it be possible for Twila and Martel to go to Area 52 and meet the young man who broke in?" Kat looked directly at the Fae Queen, more confident in her ability to speak up in front of everyone now she had the meeting this morning. She knew at the meeting earlier she had suggested they send Calliope to Area 52, but Kat had reassessed her choice and knew that only three people at the table knew she had.

"Why those two?" asked Queen Nemea.

"Martel, as you know, is adept at putting people at ease; he may glean more information from Chaos' lackey. Twila has a different skill set which could prove helpful." Katya was not about to reveal that Twila could track magic in many circumstances, but the Fae Queen would understand her meaning.

"Also, sorry to interrupt." Katya's cousin, Calliope spoke up. "Was wondering if your Majesty—" She inclined her head to the Nymph Queen. "Would you be able to check the records of all the portals in your region to see if or when Eidyia used them and if she was with anyone?"

Katya dropped her head for a moment to hide the hint of a smirk. *Brilliant*, she thought to herself. Now Nemea had something to focus on rather than bickering with King Erebus, and it insinuated why this detail hadn't been seen to by now. After all, they all knew the renegade Nymph Eidyia had been one of Chaos' biggest supporters.

"Of course, the Nymph's and Vila will make every effort to uncover anything we can regarding Eidyia and her movements." Katya watched as a calculated look crossed the Nymph's face and instantly knew where this was going. She decided to head off any further arguments by getting in first. Kat quickly turned to the Dragon King. "And, of course, you will need to go through all of your records to uncover anything suspicious that could link who broke into your Garden and stole your key."

"Of course," he grumbled with little conviction.

"Excellent," Queen Stellamaris said to no one in particular. "The question still remains on where to keep the final key."

"Put it somewhere we have already been," suggested Twila.

"Like where?" asked Jazlynn.

"Martel and I found a box that looked like a book in Eidyia's house." She turned to Nemea. "Did you find the Nymph Gem in something like that?"

"Well, yes, I did."

"And you took the gem but left everything just the same?"

"Yes."

"I gave the box to Bessander. Do you know where it is now?"

"It won't take me long to find out."

"Good." Twila smiled as she looked around the room. Katya returned the smile, though she had no idea what Twila was going to suggest. "We get the box, put the gem in it, and put it back in Eidyia's bookcase. Then we set up camp next to the cabin with soldiers from Fae, Vila, and Nymph ranks and go about investigating, like we are still looking for clues about Eidyia. Chaos will see us there, ask questions, and as far as he knows, there is only an empty box that should contain the gem but doesn't."

"That's brilliant!" Martel exclaimed. Kat watched as he reached under the table to squeeze his fiancé's hand with encouragement.

"I'm glad you think so, because it is my recommendation that instead of you going to visit the Keeper with me, you should be the one in charge of the camp at Eidyia's place. You deal with Vila and Nymph all day and will be able to smooth out any issues that may arise while investigating."

"Who will go with you to talk to the would-be thief that Chaos sent?" he asked.

"I think Julian may be of some use in that department. He is able to put people at ease very quickly. He should probably be wherever Trell is too, as only now he is uncovering his abilities as a Druid."

Katya watched as most people around the table nodded at the suggestion.

"Any objections to what Twila proposes?" asked Queen Stellamaris.

No one spoke.

"Good. Let's get this set up first thing tomorrow morning. We must make haste as we continue to play catch up with Chaos' plans."

Chapter 4
Calliope

Calliope barely suppressed her groan of annoyance as they walked out the conference room to find Apollo, Latrell, and Julian, all standing near the doorway, clearly waiting for them to be finished.

"Lord Apollo, we leave for the Dragon Garden in ten minutes, stay here," Erebus, the Dragon King, ordered.

"Yes, Your Majesty." Apollo inclined his head in agreement.

Calliope watched the powerful, tall dragon in his human form stride down the corridor and quickly catch up with the Fae Queen and Nymph Queen, who all stepped into Stellamaris' private office.

"I have a favor to ask before I return to Scarlett to seek further answers in the Area 52 library," Trell addressed the group in general.

Calliope was not surprised when Jazlynn turned to face Katya, allowing her to answer. Clearly, she still thought of herself as a member of the squad and answering to Kat, rather than the heir to the throne and the one with the true power in this circle of powerful people. It made Calliope respect Jaz even more. Though she had no intention of ever telling her that.

"What is it you need?" Kat asked.

"I would like to see the room where the crown was stolen from. You say there are pictures on the walls in all four areas the items were kept. I would like to see those pictures for myself."

"At this point, I can't see why not. You should have spoken up earlier, you could have accompanied us to the Oracle's court," Kat answered.

"Are the drawings the same?" Trell asked.

"Yes, as far as I can tell." It was Cael who answered.

He had seen three out of the four secret places of the hidden items. Only Kat had seen the one within the large pool under the mountains that contained the Dragon's Garden. Kat studied Cael for a moment; she wanted to trust him for Jaz's sake, but all she could see was the hurt he had caused and that he had the chance to hand himself in years prior and warn them about Chaos rather than choose to hide.

"Anyone else want to see it as this will be your last chance?" Kat announced.

Kat began to walk toward the wing of the house with Jaz, Cael, Julian, Twila, Martel, and Latrell following behind. By instinct, Calliope took up the rear-guard position. As she passed the waiting Lord Apollo, he grabbed her hand and held her back. "You're not going to bother saying good-bye?" he asked quietly.

"I'm still annoyed with you," she hissed, yanking her arm away.

"It's nice to know you care so much." He attempted to flirt with her, but she returned his charming look with a scathing one.

"The only thing I care about is making that bitch pay," Calliope snarled. All her pent-up anger at the Dragon Princess seeping through as it seemed Artemis would get away with her murder attempt on the Fae.

Calliope. It rankled deeper than what she wanted people to know.

Apollo reached out and took her hand and squeezed it quickly. He bent down so his mouth was close to her ear. "She will pay. You will just have to trust me, sunshine." Before Calliope had a chance to pull away, he softly kissed her cheek before straightening to his full, towering height.

"We'll see," was her only response.

The brown-haired Wyvern bowed deeply ,and as he came up, he gave her a wink, his wet sand colored, reptilian-like eyes were full of mischief, which made her insides warm.

"If you ever need a sparring partner, send a message," he challenged her in his normal louder voice.

This made her laugh; it seemed she couldn't stay angry with him for long. Calliope knew that he was referring to either type of sparring partner. "I'll wait until the bruises I gave you heal, teddy bear," she replied saucily before blowing him a kiss and hustling down the large corridor to catch up with the squad. She found Julian lagging at the back of the group. He looked relieved when she came around the corner.

"Everything okay?" he asked quietly.

"Yup," she answered lightly.

"Have I done something wrong?" Julian pressed, keeping his voice low.

She resisted the urge to roll her eyes. "Nope. Relax, Chipmunk."

"But..."

The word stopped her walking, and she yanked him into the nearest doorway. Calliope grabbed the front of his t-shirt, pulling him down so their faces were even and mere inches apart. He leered at her, an alluring smile on his beautiful face.

"You are hot, and I thank you for last night, but if you hadn't noticed, there is kinda a lot going on and I have a job to do. Get your shit together, Druid boy. You wanted to be part of this world." His face fell. *God damn it, what is it with sulky men?* She felt bad for a split second, but just as quickly shook it off. Calliope let go of his shirt and patted his chest before walking away. "Let's go."

Julian was quiet and kept a respectful distance as they hurried down the hallway to catch up with the group. They arrived in time to find an elderly warlock opening the magically locked door. As he finished and stepped away, Calliope caught the look of distrust that slid over his face as his eyes moved to Cael. She worried for Jazlynn, but not for the thief who had stolen the Fae Queen's crown. Let him suffer the ire of others for the pain he brought.

"If that will be all, Your Highness?" The warlock bowed to Jaz.

An awkward silence grew around them. Jaz looked to Katya, who shrugged.

Jazlynn inclined her head to the old warlock, thanked him, and dismissed him. They all shuffled past the giant Elven warrior statues on either side of the door and into the semi-darkened room. "They will appear brighter if we close the door," suggested Katya.

"Whatever you say." Jaz again deferred to Kat.

Calliope rolled her eyes at Jaz. Without being asked, she closed the door, but quickly opened it, before closing it again. "Just checking that we aren't going to be locked in," she said cheerfully. She allowed her eyes to adjust to the darkness before turning to face the pictures on the walls.

At that exact moment, Jazlynn gasped.

"What is it?" Cael asked.

"Nothing," she laughed it off. "I was startled by someone brushing passed my arm. Very funny, Calliope," Jaz explained.

Calliope laughed and silently stepped closer to the silhouette of Jaz. "You got me; though I didn't think you'd react like that. Sorry, everyone, bad joke." She covered for Jaz, but wondered what had made the princess react in such a way.

"It's always you two," Kat said half-jokingly. "Can we all focus on the pictures now?"

"I know why he wants the Keeper's Tome," Trell said slowly. Calliope turned her head to see him. He didn't look at anyone, just continued to study the faintly glowing picture of two trees with their branches twisted together to make an arch. "He thinks it holds the secrets of the Angels."

"Does it?" asked Calliope.

"No, but it is linked to another. It holds the secrets of the Keeper, making it specific to the complex that is Area 52 and all they protect within it, and focuses mostly on witch and warlock magic. I think he hopes that it will give him further information regarding the other book."

"So there really is an Angel's book?" Calliope asked.

"Yes, it was stolen from heaven by the Angel who fell in love with Devlin who became Chaos. I managed to get it from them, and it was kept in a secret location, until Caesar took France, and the ancient Druid Library was uncovered. I took the only two books I was instructed to and went into hiding."

Julian whistled. "Man, you are old. That happened in 121 BC."

Trell nodded and there was approval in his eyes. "You remember things like that?"

"Yeah, I have a knack for it."

"It is a skill of the Druids. An eidetic memory it is now called, but you would have been known as a Lore Master in ancient times."

"So, let me guess; the two books you took for safe-keeping were this Angel book and the Keeper's book? What did you do with the Angel book?" asked Calliope.

"Gave it to the safe-keeper of the Elves of the Sol Court."

"And Chaos knows about it?"

"Yes, though he was captured during the War of Elves and never found it."

"That explains why Chaos is so invested in trying to get into the Elven Ingress," Katya spoke. "As all portals were destroyed during the War of Elves, there is now only one way in."

"No, hang on," interrupted Twila. She turned to Cael. "Didn't you say that you hid for quite some time in the Elven Plane?"

"Yes."

"If there are no portals, then how did you get there?" Twila asked.

"There is a portal. It's on the boundary between Shifter territory and the Nymph Realm. I can sense portals as they take power from the leylines to anchor in place," he explained.

"Shit," Trell swore. "There are only two people alive who know how to create portals. That's Devlin and myself, and I didn't create that portal."

"So, he could be creating portals everywhere he goes?" asked Julian.

"No, no, it's not that simple," Trell spoke rapidly. "They take much effort, time, preparation, and magic to create. Leylines must meet in a certain pattern and be stable enough in both Planes to sustain magical energy feeding into it. After the fall of the Elven Empire, much of the magics on Plane four went wild and there were immense aftershocks and severe backlash from the powerful magics that had been released by so many races. The leylines could not absorb all the power and the portals failed as they were either overloaded or deprived of the magical source. Plus, he was supposedly stripped of his powers when he was thrown into hell."

Calliope had watched the entire exchange and noted that Trell hadn't taken his eyes off the etching of the two trees that created an arch. "You know where that gate is, don't you?" she asked.

"Yes, it's the Troll's Doorway in Ireland. It's where the Druid's would have their ceremonies. It is where Arella and Devlin first met, and she carried the Angel's Scriptures with her that day. She read from it to test us. There was an altar in front of the trees with an amber stone on it."

Something clicked in Calliope's mind. "The Oracle's dagger had an amber stone in its hilt."

"Each key unlocks a gate," Trell reminded everyone.

"The Oracle's Dagger unlocks the Troll's Doorway."

"And my guess is that the Fae Queens crown opens the Elven Ingress," Julian added.

"Why?" asked Jaz and Calliope at the same time.

"The Fae Queen's crown was a gift from the Elves at the end of the war."

Calliope was impressed with Julian's knowledge. Maybe there was more to Chipmunk than she had first thought.

"What does it look like?" asked Trell.

Jaz answered, "Shards of crystal with a larger piece in the middle with a crescent moon carved into it."

"The crown of the Court of Shadows looked as you describe," said Trell.

"I wonder which one of these two the Dragon Ring unlocks," mused Calliope as she turned her attention to the final two pictures. One had a path with waves on either side going in between two large pillars. Each rectangle shaped pillar had seven circles vertically placed along its front. The other gate looked more like what you would find at a medieval castle. It had a portcullis style grill gate, surrounded by large blocks of stone.

"The castle-looking gate is tied to the Dragon Ring," Trell said softly, almost reverently. "The gate sits in the French Alps. It was part of the Druid's Library, but it was not something I ever used or took much notice of as it wasn't part of my role as a Druid."

"Why is it called the Dragon's Ring?" Julian asked.

"It was in the possession of the Pendragons for many years and picked up its nickname then. One of the Elven Kings wanted it returned to its rightful place, so a deal was struck with King Arthur. I was there when the ring was returned. It is only now that I know the ring and the gate are linked."

Calliope was impressed. While the other Fae of her squad knew enough human lore to get by, she had spent many years on Plane two perfecting different forms of martial arts and living amongst the humans.

"You got to meet Arthur Pendragon?"

"I did. And he was kind and intimidating all at once."

"I have no clue who you are talking about," admitted Kat. "What I want to know is where the gate is in the Enchanted Underworld?"

"How do you know that's the one that leads here?" Twila asked before Calliope could.

"Because I know that one—" Kat waved her hand at the two rectangle pillars with the path running through. "Is the gate to the Ghosts Avenue."

"And you know where it is?" asked Julian excitedly.

"Yes, but I am not at liberty to discuss that."

Calliope's mind was racing as she took in all the facts. She quickly came to the conclusion that Jaz also knew where the gate to the Ghosts Avenue was and that was what the little gasp had been about. Well, if Jaz and Kat didn't want everyone knowing Calliope would not question them further, they would tell her when they could or needed to. "Okay, so the Dragon Ring Gate leads to the Third Plane, but how do we find it here?" She shifted the subject back.

Everyone was silent. Calliope knew she was still missing something important, but it sat too far back in her mind for her to reach. Unexpectedly she got a flashback of the moment the last of her breath escaped her body and she began to sink to the bottom of the Dragon's Garden pool. Calliope knew it was the silence of this room combined with the darkness and glowing pictures triggering her. Something nagged at her as she struggled with her living nightmare. Calliope held her breath without realizing it, and as her lungs burned for release, her mind screamed just like it did as the Elven statues in the pool floated into view before everything went dark.

A hand on her back startled Calliope, pulling her out of her trance-like state. She expelled her breath in a rush.

"You, okay?" asked Julian.

She wanted to say no. She wanted to cling to him and have him wipe her unshed tears. But that was weakness, and they had no time for it. Instead, she stepped forward, away from the caring hand on the small of her back.

"Of course I am, Druid boy," she said sarcastically. Everyone had turned to look at them in the dim light of the glowing drawings. "Well, now I have everyone's attention." She laughed.

"Forever the attention seeker," Jaz commented.

"You know me," Calliope scoffed. "No seriously, I think I might have something. We have all been to different locations of the gates and keys, and at every one I can think of, there were Elven warrior statues. Can anyone say otherwise?"

"Damn, that is clever," said Jaz.

Chapter 5
Jazlynn

It was late and the wide hallway was empty as the squad of Weapons walked to their rooms. The four women walked in silence, Jaz slightly in front. She was feeling a little out of sorts as the ramifications of Cael's betrayal and her own responsibilities weighed heavily on her. The other three Weapons in her squad were being sent out to find or check on gates, while she would be stuck in the capital playing go-between. The mood in the corridor was heavy with everyone thinking of their upcoming assignment. Jaz was desperate for a little spark of the carefree kinship she shared with these women to take her mind off a conversation she knew she had to have tonight.

As Jaz reached the first door of the four suites, she turned and cleared her throat to get everyone's attention. "You know what I can't figure out?" She paused for dramatic effect. Calliope, Kat, and Twila all stopped to look at her. A wicked grin appeared on her face, and she couldn't help herself. "I can't figure out which of the two tall handsome men that hang on your every word you are sleeping with." Jaz looked directly at Calliope as if to challenge her in denying she wasn't doing something with one of them.

"Well, let me contribute a little more to the mystery," Kat interrupted.

Jaz caught the surreptitious poke that Calliope aimed at her cousin's rib cage and laughed. Calliope was clearly hiding something.

"Oh, come on, let's not pick on Calli," Twila spoke up.

"Yeah, give me a break." Calliope smiled cheekily and stepped behind Twila as if she needed protecting. "What did I ever do to you guys?"

This brought a groan from Twila, and she stepped out of the way. "You're on your own with that stupid statement."

Calliope attempted to look like the jibe had hurt her feelings. Jaz didn't believe it for a second. "Spill with the gossip, Kat," she encouraged.

"Let's just say that one of them calls her sunshine and the other was standing there shirtless and had given her that cut lip."

"Tattletale," Calliope said.

"Oh, this is too much," laughed Jaz. She opened her door and waved at her squad, feeling better for the teasing of her friend and the camaraderie they shared. "Night, Kat. Night. Twila. Night, sunshine," Jaz called as she hurried through the door before Calliope could find something to throw at her.

"You'll keep, Princess," Calliope growled as the door swung shut.

Jaz turned to find Cael sitting on the bed, fully clothed with an anxious look on his handsome face, his beautiful hazel eyes sad. Cael held out his hand and she walked toward him. Jaz felt something shift and her few moments of merriment dissipated, replaced by resignation that she knew they couldn't ignore the situation no matter how much they wished it differently.

"I'm sorry," he said softly as he took her hand and pulled her to sit beside him on the bed.

Jaz allowed herself to be drawn down. "About what?" she asked. It wasn't what she had expected him to say.

"It's my fault that you are being kept here instead of being sent out into the field with the other Weapons."

"Not your doing at all," she assured him, though Jazlynn wasn't quite as certain as she pretended to be.

"They don't trust me," he admitted, his voice quiet but pained.

Jaz squeezed his hand while reaching out to skim her thumb across his cheek. "I wish I could tell you differently, but I agree."

Cael brought his free hand up to cover hers, bringing her palm to his lips where he kissed it. "If only I could go back and start again. None of this may be happening if I had just told you what they were after."

"What's done is done," Jaz said quietly. "Wishing won't change anything but make us more frustrated. I've noticed that you've been quiet at the meetings. Is it because you have nothing to say or feel your voice is not welcome?"

He shrugged noncommittally.

"Is there something you want to add? I can always bring it up," Jaz asked.

Cael continued to sit there. "I'm so sorry," he repeated.

"I meant is there something you want to bring up or add at the council meeting that you would like me to say for you."

"Yes, I know." His voice was small. "I just can't help but feel that I'll never be able to redeem myself."

A horrible idea began to form, and no matter how much Jaz tried to push it aside, she couldn't. The thought had taken on a life of its own, and her insecurities fed into it with full force. Jaz began to spiral with what if's and second guesses. Did he really want to be with her or was he here because the alternative was prison? While he was with her, he had some form of freedom. The idea made Jazlynn sick, and she couldn't shake it. She slowly pulled her hand away and stood, putting some distance between them.

"What are you doing?" His voice carried an edge to it that she had not heard before.

"You promised no more secrets, but I get the feeling you are still holding things back."

"I figured out that the warrior statues were in every location where a gate or key is kept but didn't want to say it..." His voice trailed off. "Because I feel everyone's eyes on me; judging me when I speak." Cael stood and closed the gap she had created. "I understand why. I would feel the same if the situation was reversed, but it doesn't make it any easier. All the side glances and underlying hostility make me feel like I can't contribute properly."

Jaz took his hand and pulled him close. "I wish I could make it better, but you and I both know the only thing that will fix this is time and you being transparent about everything."

Cael gathered her up in his arms and kissed her softly on the forehead. "I can live with everyone else's distrust but not yours." He kissed the tip of her nose. "But it breaks my heart every time you begin to pull away from me and it kills me to know I brought it all on myself." He kissed her cheek. "Promise you won't pull away. Instead, keep telling me how you feel."

Jaz tilted her head and looked up into his earnest handsome face. The full lips, broad forehead and square jaw still gave her butterflies. "I will try not to pull away, but it's hard sometimes. I'm worried about many things at the moment."

He kissed her upturned lips. A soft, gentle brush of his mouth was all it took to send a shiver down her spine. "I don't know what my future looks like. I had never really thought about being anything other than a Weapon since you stole the crown."

Cael kissed her again. This time his lips hovered over hers as he spoke. "I don't know, I think with your abilities Kirkpatrick always had you marked for Weapons training. In the end, I probably just gave you more motivation."

She'd never really thought about it like that. All the training before Katya, Twila, and Calliope had shown up had not been simply because Weapons Master Kirkpatrick had been looking to fill his time. Had her father, General Owen, always meant for her to be trained to join the Weapons of the Fae Queen squad?

"Mmm," was her reply as he kissed her again.

Cael moved his head and began to kiss and nip her neck, moving down to her shoulder. Jaz moved her head to the other side, showing him that she was receptive to what he was doing. Cael reached out and took hold of her shoulders, and as he turned her to face away from him, he continued to trail kisses around neck. He lifted her blonde curls to one side and placed his fingertips on her exposed tattoo at the nape of her neck.

"Promise me that there are no more secrets," Jaz said.

The room stilled and Jaz held her breath. She felt Cael lift his fingers from her neck and pause. She had been trained to notice things like this, she didn't need to be facing him to know he hesitated for a moment. Ever so gently, Jaz felt him press his lips to her tattoo. She reached out and took Cael's hand and brought his arm around and across her face until his wrist, with its matching tattoo, was in front of her. She kissed it, feeling his pulse race against her lips.

"I love you," he said softly as he found the zip to the hot pink gown, with its tight bodice and flowing skirt. Inch by inch he tugged the zip down. With great care he pulled the dress over her head, avoiding her wings.

Jaz turned and quickly slipped out of her knickers as Cael lay her dress over the back of a chair. Instead of undressing him, she chose to sit on another chair, leaning back into the soft cushions, opening her legs ever so slightly to expose a mere hint of herself. Jaz bit her lower lip in anticipation as Cael's eyes lit up and he smiled like a predator as he quickly undressed, not bothering to pick up his clothes. He left them in a pile beside his feet. He unexpectedly fell to his hands and knees and crawled toward her. Jaz's core burst into flames as she watched him stalk toward her.

Cael picked up her foot and sucked each toe, running his hand up and down her calf and each time inching a little higher. He let her foot go and began to kiss his way across her ankle and up her calf. As he reached her thigh he ran his tongue up her inner leg, making her shake at the soft delicious feel of him.

Jaz opened her legs, allowing him to continue his tongue all the way up. Cael didn't stop until he reached her clit. He gently took it between his teeth and sucked, eliciting a moan from Jaz.

"Don't stop," she urged.

Without taking his mouth away, he reached up and brought both her legs over his shoulders as he kneeled in front of her, his face buried between her thighs. His tongue swirled around her clit, time and time again, and Jaz reached out, grasping his short brown hair in her fist, holding his face in place as she began to grind against him. Cael kept the pressure perfect, sucking and licking as he allowed her to rub against him. Quickly her orgasm grew and just before she was going to tumble over the edge, he would lessen the pressure, and she would moan in protest before he once again brought her close but allowed her no release.

Frustrated, Jaz let go of his hair and moved her legs so she could reach down and pull him up by lifting under his arms. Cael looked up from her clit and grinned wickedly before lowering his head to kiss his way up her stomach. He raised himself up on his knees and she wrapped her legs around his waist. He rested his cock against her for mere seconds before he started to ease into her. Slowly Cael pushed in before withdrawing just as slowly, only to push into her a few inches more. It was mind blowing and frustrating all at the same time, and Jazlynn loved every moment of it.

Jaz pushed her crossed feet down, forcing him deeper. She grinned in satisfaction as a groan escaped him.

"So hot," he murmured as his mouth claimed her nipple. As his tongue teased her nipple, he continued to fuck her with exquisite leisurely strokes, slowly rolling his hips when he couldn't go any further and rubbing himself against her. Cael moved over and over again, with each stroke telling her how beautiful, special, and kind she was, and how much he loved her.

With every movement, Jaz's breath grew more ragged. She focused on the growing sensations in her core and tensed herself against him, making him groan louder. She didn't think there was anything hotter than making a man moan.

"Come for me, baby," Jaz urged.

"You first," he managed to get out.

She pushed her feet against his arse again and again, making him pick up the pace.

"Together," she said.

"Together," he agreed.

He lowered his lips to her, and she opened her mouth to him. Their tongues danced around each other as they continued to fuck harder and faster, both racing to orgasm.

"Yes," was all Jaz could say as she fell over the edge of heaven and her body quivered as the orgasm took her. Her body clenched around him as she rode the wave of pleasure, drawing out his own body-shaking orgasm. They both slowed their movements, cherishing the beautiful sensations of them joined together until they stilled, depleted but satisfied.

While Cael snored softly beside her, Jaz's mind raced. Her thoughts circled in on each other in a jumbled mess. She couldn't push the daunting unwanted thoughts away anymore.

Remaining a Weapon was looking less likely, as her position as the Queen's preferred heir was becoming more and more common knowledge amongst the nobility of the Enchanted Underworld. As her thoughts shied away from the massive life changes her being named heir brought up, Jaz tried to think happy thoughts. She kept away from thinking about what was going to happen between her and Cael when she became Queen. If they had children, they would not be allowed to rule as they would not be pure blood Fae. Would she even be allowed to marry him and he be named consort or would that be forbidden?

"Ugggh," she muttered as she changed positions and flipped over to her other side, now facing Cael.

Jaz resisted the urge to trace Cael's features with her hand as she gazed at him. In the end, she gave in and reached out to touch his hair. As her mind continued to torture her with unwanted memories and thoughts, Jaz recalled Cael's moment of hesitation earlier.

"What are you hiding?" she whispered. "Please don't break my heart again; I don't think I could recover a second time."

Chapter 6
Twila

It had been a long and exhausting day, and Twila was grateful for not having to go any further than her usual suite in the palace for a hot shower and to seek her bed. Typically, staying in the palace rather than the barracks when they were in the capital made Twila uncomfortable. She often forgot that one of her dearest friends was a Princess of the Fae; to her, Jazlynn was a trusted friend, colleague, and roommate. It was only in the palace, when people continually bowed and looked to her, was it put front and center; and the more this mission went on, the less of a warrior Jaz became and more of a royal.

Twila didn't want to think about the changes that would come too soon if she was reading everything right. Today had seen so much revealed already, that for now, all she wanted was to be held and turn her mind off before tomorrow's mission began. Turning the shower off, Twila took a large, soft white towel and dried herself, thinking of nothing more than how fluffy and luxurious the towel felt against her skin. She quickly rubbed lotion on her face and body. She spun a silk short robe in her customary white around her body, with slits in the back for her wings to pop out from. When she climbed into bed, she would wrap her wings around her torso like she usually did, making them almost invisible.

Quickly Twila tidied the bathroom. She knew there were servants who would do it tomorrow, but it was against her nature to be untidy. She tucked her feet into white slippers before grabbing the tube of hand cream and emerging from the bathroom.

"Better?" Martel asked as he smiled from the armchair he was sitting in. He put the small journal down that he wrote in every night and stood, stretching his arms overhead.

"Much. Though I think I could sleep for a week. So much is happening so fast. I feel like I can't catch my breath." Twila walked to her side of the bed and took off her beautiful new engagement ring, marveling at how it sparkled as she placed it in the box she had received it in. "So pretty," she said softly as she squeezed a large dollop of hand cream onto her palm and began to rub it in.

Martel finished his stretching and came to stand on his side of the bed. "Why put it back in the box?" he asked, his head nodding toward the bedside table.

"We have to be nondescript. I turn up with that gorgeous rock on my hand and someone will remember it. I would also hate for it to get lost or broken."

It was easy to tell by the look on his face that Martel was hurt, but he paused before answering. "You are only going to Area 52, so what is the harm in wearing the ring?" he pointed out.

Twila stared at him for a moment, before she responded, as she didn't want to hurt his feelings either. It appeared they were both being extra careful with their words tonight.

"How long have we been together? And how many times have I been called away from one assignment and put on another or the assignment changes as more information is discovered?" She tried to sound reasonable.

"I know, it's just—" He stopped and turned away from her, pulling the bed sheets down and climbing into bed.

"Just what?" she urged.

"Doesn't matter. I will get over it."

Rather than retort with a sharp comment or push him further, Twila silently tugged the sheet down on her side, trying to come up with a solution. "Will you keep it safe for me?" she asked.

"I have kept it safe for you this long," he said softly, settling onto his pillow.

"True, but can you carry it with you and not just put it away somewhere safe? Then a piece of me is with you until we meet again. And when you return it each time, it will be like I carry a piece of you around."

"So, we share your bridal ring?" He turned to face her, his face earnest and handsome.

She nodded as she took the ring back out of its box and crawled onto the bed.

"Sit up," she said.

Martel did what he was told. Twila climbed onto his lap, straddling him. She smiled shyly as she reached out and undid the necklace around his neck. Without speaking, she threaded the necklace through the ring before placing it back around his neck. "There," Twila spoke softly. "I'm close to your heart."

She couldn't say more as she struggled to find the words that would not make her cry. Would it always be like this? Their joining together for a few days of bliss and then being pulled apart by commitments that neither wanted to resign from? Twila didn't want to give up her position as a Weapon, and Martel didn't want to stop being a diplomat. This was the life they both loved but each time they parted it got harder.

Martel took Twila by her shoulders and pulled her gently towards him. They rested their foreheads against each other. "Ring or no ring," he spoke in a whisper. "You are my heart. Always come back to me."

Twila softly pressed her lips to his. "I promise."

T wila snuggled deeper into the crook of Martel's arm, content and sleepy. "*Twila?*" A voice whispered in her head. She knew it was Jaz.

"Yes?"

"*I need to meet with you, but you can't tell anyone. Are you okay with that?*"

"*Of course.*"

"*I'll be in the grotto. Can you be there in half an hour?*"

"*I'll do my best. Just need to wait for Martel to fall asleep properly.*"

"*Okay.*"

Twila felt the presence of Princess Jazlynn leave her mind. She continued to lie still like nothing had happened, but now her thoughts raced—all sleepiness having evaporated. What did Jaz want and why did she want no one to know about it? Twila understood the need for secrecy, but to exclude their leader, Katya, and their squad mate, Calliope, was something Jaz had never done before. It made Twila feel uncomfortable, but she trusted Jaz implicitly, so if that's what the heir to the throne asked of her, Twila would readily agree. But as she lay listening to her fiancé's breathing deepen, her mind turned over every possible reason why Jaz wanted to meet. She didn't like the answers she came up with.

Chapter 7

Jazlynn

Frustration bubbled inside her as the yoke that now kept her stuck on this realm tightened even further with the appearance of her father, General Owen. She prayed he was not going to stop her. Jaz and Cael were about to enter the building that housed the sigil room, which would take them to the Nymph's Realm. Cael assured her that it was the closest sigil to the newly discovered portal. Nemea and Martel had already gone ahead to start preparing for the fake investigation around Eidyia's house so they could hide the final key, the Nymph's Gem, in its original box there.

With her father's arrival came a squad of twenty Fae soldiers.

"They better not be here to protect me." It was a clear statement and not framed as a question. Jaz used talking marks with her fingers when she said "protect me."

"No one is here to protect you. I am well aware of your capabilities. However, I don't think it wise to have only you two going through the portal to see if everything is well," her father said briskly. "Half the squad is to accompany you; the other half will be placed under the command of Ambassador Martel."

Everyone standing within hearing distance knew what he really meant. Though it wasn't spoken aloud, it was clear that he didn't want her out in the Enchanted Underworld with just Cael. The most powerful warlock in the Seven Planes was most assuredly not to be trusted.

She narrowed her eyes at the General and was about to mind speak him just what she thought of that idea when Cael interrupted.

"I think that's smart, Jaz. We should take them with us. They will need to stand guard on both sides once we leave, as we can't know if Chaos is using the portal to come and go as he pleases." He spoke in a reasonable voice and gave her a pleading look that clearly asked her to not argue with her father over him.

Jaz clamped her mouth shut. Damn both of them and their reasonableness. She was a Weapon of the Fae Queen and unnamed heir to the Crystal

Throne—she couldn't be seen having a tantrum because she couldn't get her own way.

"Both valid points," she conceded graciously. "We might get a lucky break and catch one of his underlings if we don't get him."

General Owen nodded his agreement.

"Form up," he ordered the patrol.

Without any further discussion, the Fae warriors formed an orderly line behind the sigil that would transport them to the sigil room in the Nymph and Vila's palace. With a silent salute to the General, one by one they stepped onto the sigil which would glow in warning before they vanished.

Soon the sigil room was empty apart from Cael, Jazlynn, and her father.

"You next." He nodded to Cael.

"Yes, Sir." Cael didn't wait. He hurried onto the sigil and gave Jaz a tight smile before he disappeared.

Ignoring protocol and with no one but a few of the normal guards around to see, General Owen became the concerned father that he never showed anyone but the immediate family. He gave Jaz a warm embrace and gently stroked her hair like she was five again.

"I hope you know what you're doing," he muttered as he lowered his head to kiss her cheek.

"I trust him," she murmured back as she returned his cheek kiss with one of her own.

"And I trust you." He squeezed her one final time before releasing her and stepping back.

Jaz reached out with her mind and spoke softly through the link she created between them.

"*Love you, Dad,*" she said with her mind speech abilities.

"*Love you too,*" he responded.

Jaz saluted the General, becoming all business again, and walked onto the sigil that would take her to the Nymph Queen's palace. Within two heart-beats, she was gone from the sigil room within the walls of the temple and had appeared in the small space that Twila had been in only a few days ago when she had come to investigate the renegade Nymph, Eidyia.

Before moving out of the room, Jaz took a deep, steadying breath and prayed to any god that was listening that her plan was going to work. She patted her pocket to make certain the square gem that Chaos was chasing was still there and put a pleasant and confident smile on her face.

"Welcome," Baron Martel spoke as she walked into the small waiting room and through it to find her guards flanking each side of the corridor. "This way." He gestured down the hall. "We will skip all the for-malities and head straight out." He spoke normally, but without giving anything away.

"Works for me," she answered. Jaz smiled reassuringly at Cael as she met him at the end of the line of guards. He fell in behind the Ambassador and Princess.

Without preamble, Jaz walked beside Martel as she noted they walked through the back entrances to everything. It didn't take them long to be out in the garden near the Crystal Lake that all Nymphs loved to live nearby. Once they were outside, it was less likely for them to be overhead.

"Did she give you the box?" Jaz asked Martel, again not being specific about anything. They both knew that she was referring to the book that had a secret compartment that had once held the Nymph Gem.

"Yes."

"Good."

"Has everything been set up for you to continue your investigation of the rogue Nymph?" she asked loudly.

"Camp is being established out the front of Eidyia's cabin and we will continue our questioning of her neighbors while we search her cabin thoroughly," Martel replied just as loudly.

"Good," she nodded.

They reached the servant entrance to the Nymph palace gardens and stepped through.

"Well, this is where we part." Jaz held out her hand, and the Ambassador took it. He palmed the

Nymph Gem Chaos was searching for and released her hand. He casually placed his hand in his pocket. Jaz nodded at two of her guards. "You and you, please escort Ambassador Martel to his destination and then rejoin us."

They both saluted her and fell in behind Martel. He waved before turning and heading down the path to the renegade Nymph's small house.

"Shall we?" she said brightly as she turned to Cael and gestured toward the East.

"Yes," he answered. "Are you sure you will be able to follow me?"

"Now that you aren't covering your mind, I should be able to find you if you don't go too far ahead at a time," she explained again. Jaz turned to the squad of eighteen guards. "We have permission to transform within the Nymph Realm. Please do so."

It was a sight that Jaz would never tire of as she watched as all eighteen warriors unfurled their iridescent torso armor to reveal varying colors and styles of perfect Fae wings. They fluttered the wings to lift themselves off the ground and began to spin in the air, faster and faster until they were a blur of color. It was over quickly and as they slowed their spinning they had transformed into their true form. A tiny, no more than the size of an average thumbnail, glittery fairy.

Everyone hovered in place as Jaz unfurled her own beautiful pink wings and rose from the ground. She loved this moment of transformation. It took mere seconds, but the freeing feeling of her true self was bliss. The only issue with being this tiny was the fairies could not communicate well with other species, but Jaz's mind speech powers gave her the advantage.

"*Ready?*" She sent the thought to Cael.

"*Let's go. I think no more than ten distance leaps should do this,*" he thought back. Without any further warnings or discussion, Cael vanished.

Jaz kept the link to Cael open, and after a few moments, pushed the thought out. "*Cael?*"

"*I'm here.*"

"*Sing to me.*"

"*As my lady wishes.*"

Jaz smiled to herself as his strong voice began to sing a corny romantic court song.

"*Really?*" she asked as she began to fly toward his mind's voice. The patrol of fairies followed.

"*It's the only one I remember all the words to,*" he admitted.

It didn't take them more than fifteen minutes to arrive at a small copse of trees to find him leaning against one.

Two hours later and Jaz was more than over the soppy love song. They had arrived at the border between the Nymph Realm and the Lunara Vale. The road had been left behind several kilometres prior and they were standing between the softer, more sparsely vegetated landscape of the Nymphs and the darker, heavily pine treed beginnings of the Lunara Forest, that surrounded the vale where most of the Witches and Warlocks resided.

Jaz quickly transformed back into her human shape and created dark pink tight pants, a tight black t-shirt, and Doc Martin boots and brought in her wings to wrap around her mid-section that looked like a cute sparkly pink vest but that was hard armour. By the time she settled onto the earth, the patrol of warriors were all spinning in place and transforming back into the usual size and Fae Warrior uniforms.

"Where's the portal?" she asked, looking around.

"A few minutes walk into the forest. It's between two lilac geranium plants."

"What do they look like?" asked one of the soldiers.

"Palm-shaped leaves with loose clusters of showy light purple flowers," Cael explained as he moved into the forest with Jaz following.

Jaz nodded. "Search the ground as we walk. Be careful where you step. We are looking for footprints or paw prints around this area. Any unusual activity."

They found nothing of consequence by the time Carl halted a stop in front of two small shrubs of pretty purple flowers.

"How do you want to do this, Your Highness?" Captain Athertonne asked.

"Pick five warriors to go through first. Let's do it in rapid succession so if there is anyone on the other side they won't have a chance to escape. Then I will go through and then Cael. I will send someone back through with further instructions within a few minutes. If no one comes back, send through a further eight and the rest of you go get help."

"Agreed," Captain Athertonne said. He picked out five soldiers and they lined up in front of the flowering shrubs. "Remember to keep walking when you get to the other side so no one falls on anyone as they come through."

"Yes, Sir," they all barked in unison.

Jaz and Cael moved to the back of the line and then the next emergency eight brought up the rear.

"Ready when you are Captain," she called.

"You heard her. Move out," he ordered.

Chapter 8

Twila

The book glowed a deep red to Twila's magical sight.

"It feels furious," she told them. "I've never had a book feel anything before," she explained, looking up at both of them. Twila tried to explain further. "Typically, I'll sense something, but it's always from the magic that comes through the item. When I found the box that held the Nymph Gem it made me feel queasy, like there was bile in the back of my throat. But it wasn't coming from the box but the person's magic that had held the box, which we assume was Chaos. It's never from the object. But this..." She pointed to the book, with its intriguing cover of seven circles in a vertical line, each with an embossed picture of something in its center. "This fury is actually emanating from the book itself."

Twila removed her hands and the sense of anger faded but didn't completely dissipate. It always took a while for the stronger emotions to fade from her body when she channeled her magic in this way.

The white clad Fae stood in the fabled library of Area 52 with Scarlett and Trell watching her. A large black dog, Nyx, stood next to Scarlett. The most powerful witch of her generation, also known as The Keeper, absently rested her hand on the huge beast's head.

"Fascinating," Scarlett murmured as she tilted her head to the side and studied Twila before looking at the book. "I get nothing unusual from it. It gives off power, which makes sense, as according to Trell, it's supposed to be the most powerful grimoire for my kind." She looked over to the Druid. "When Trell initially touched it it grew hot and I could feel that." Scarlett spoke to him, and Twila heard the undercurrent of accusation. "He said it was because he was a shifter, a special type. But we all now know that isn't true. Did it recognize you or your Druid blood?" she asked him pointedly.

Twila watched the two of them.

"Honestly, I don't know." Trell looked like he was going to say something more, but instead he closed his mouth and waited. Scarlett, in Twila's opinion, was trying to look professional but she was hovering between anger and hurt and struggling not to say something she shouldn't in front of others.

"Trell, would you mind touching the book while I touch it? I'd like to see if it changes response," Twila asked, hoping to get the pair back on track. The accusations and explanations were going to have to wait between the two of them.

"Good idea," he said, avoiding Scarlett's eyes. Twila almost felt sorry for him, but she wasn't about to get involved in their personal lives. Scarlett was a friend, but she was much closer to Katya than the rest of the squad. Twila would let Kat deal with the fall out of this situationship if or when this crisis was over. Trell put his hands on the book. It was a light touch, just his fingertips rested on it.

Twila didn't hesitate. She reached out and put her hand next to Trell's, and she could feel the heat emanating from it before she had physically touched it. Once her fingertips were resting on it, the intensity of ire rose. It was like Trell had raised its aggression levels.

"It is definitely increased and hot to touch. But the anger is not toward you... it feels more like a warning." Twila removed her hand as did Trell.

The anger faded again but lingered more than before, like it was clinging to her. There was an undertone of something else now. Had their combined touch triggered it? Twila closed her eyes and opened up her magical senses. It was a difficult place to center yourself as the entire building was run on magic. There were also magical beings working within the walls for the Keeper, as well as the Forgotten Ones that were imprisoned in the basement. Shutting that all out and trying to sense a single magical strand was tiring and difficult. Step by step she took the magical threads around her and pushed them to her outer senses until there were two left. They were entangled, but rather than in a difficult knot, it was if one was holding and protecting the other.

"The book is connected to another magic. It's hot because that's how it shows its anger to the Druid, but I can sense the underlying emotion," Twila explained. It was difficult to find the words for what she was experiencing, as most of it was instinctual rather than taught magic. The other Weapons in her squad were able to learn their skills with Weapons Master Kirkpatrick and a few trusted others, while Twila had to figure out much on her own, as you couldn't teach emotion and how to decipher what she felt.

"There's another thread of magic attached to the book, not emanating from it." Twila reached out her mind and spoke in her thoughts to the Keeper's Tome. "*I will take up what you protect. You can trust me,*" she promised. In her mind, she created a picture of herself holding out her hands, palms up, waiting.

The book responded with a picture of Scarlett. It was barely discernible but that is what Twila saw in her mind.

"Scarlett," she spoke quietly. "Come and place your hand on the book, please."

Scarlett didn't question the Fae. As Scarlett's fingers brushed the surface Twila heard a whisper. "Trusted?"

Was it a whisper or a mere suggestion of the word, Twila couldn't tell, but the implication was clear—could she be trusted?

"Yes," the Keeper answered both in her mind and aloud.

The book responded by unraveling itself from the final thread and allowing it to fall into the outstretched palms of Twila. It did so with a sense of urgency attached. The hot angry thread faded and evaporated back into the book.

Twila cradled the remaining thread and examined it slowly with her magic, there was something familiar about it now that it wasn't overshadowed with the protective strand.

"We've made too many assumptions, I think," she began as she opened her eyes.

"Meaning?" asked Trell.

"We are trying to play catch up and rushing to judgments." Twila was searching for something lurking at the back of her mind. "We're taking too many ideas at face value, but now we know what we are up against and how long this has been in the planning, it seems strange that this attempt to get the Keeper's Tome failed. Chaos has been ahead of us this whole time till now," she reasoned.

"Damn, you're right," said Scarlett.

"The only time he has failed is when the Nymph Queen's greed got the better of her and she took the Nymph Gem for herself—that was something Chaos couldn't anticipate." Twila continued to think aloud as she reasoned through what her subconscious was trying to sort through. She let her mind follow the strand and was quickly rewarded with a pull in the direction toward the entrance to the library. She wasn't about to follow the thread she gingerly held without knowing more.

Scarlett clicked her tongue, gaining Twila's attention and turned to Trell.

"If you knew this was the Keeper's Tome, wouldn't Chaos?"

"Well, yes," admitted the Druid.

"And if you know this book is the major grimoire for witches and warlocks, wouldn't he?" Scarlett continued. "So, why would he—"

"Bother to send someone to get a book he knew wasn't what he wanted?" Twila followed through with what she thought Scarlett was getting at.

"Fuck," Trell swore. "It makes more sense than Devlin trying to get a book that will do him no good. Shit, this is on me. I am the one that said I knew what he was after."

"No, no." Twila shook her head to emphasise that she didn't think he had caused a problem. "You warned us this was about revenge, and from what you said, it still holds up. I just think we've been focused on the Keeper's Tome when really he sent Targon for something else."

"Okay, let's start at the beginning," suggested Scarlett. "What does Chaos want?"

"He wants revenge for the death of his love, the Angel Arella," Trell answered.

"And how will he exact revenge?" Scarlett asked.

"He swore he would escape the Seventh Plane and lead the demon hordes upon the gates of heaven to crush the God that cruelly and mercilessly stripped Arella of her powers before throwing her into the mists below the Ghost's Avenue to be devoured by the demons."

"Wow… that's a powerful love," Scarlett said. Twila thought she almost sounded impressed.

It was Trell who answered. "That's not love; that's obsession and guilt. If he had loved her enough, he would have left her alone. He corrupted her with his love and desires and ego forever wanting more and then felt guilty when it all came crashing down. But instead of owning his part, he blamed everyone else and will destroy the realms of Gods and the Enchanted Ones to appease himself."

"And he has escaped the Demon Realm, though we haven't figured out how yet, and is working on opening the Gates of Ascension to reveal the Stairway to Heaven," Twila continued the narrative.

"And you open the Gates by collecting the keys which were hidden," Scarlett joined in.

"Oh My God! That's it," Twila exclaimed and looked down at the invisible magical thread still resting in the palms of her open hands. She reached out with her senses and gently formed the thought. *You're the link to the Crown?*

The thread pulsated briefly.

"He brought the crown here." Twila looked to Trell and Scarlett. "I'm going to follow the thread now I know what it is," she explained. She looked to the Keeper. "If that's okay?"

"Of course, but I have a bad feeling I know exactly where it is going to lead."

"Me too." A moment of dread filled her but she pushed it aside. There was no time for that. Her role as a Weapon allowed no room for the luxury of self doubt. Twila opened her senses entirely, trusting the thread now she knew that it was somehow linked to the Fae Queen's crown. She also now understood why the thread only revealed itself to her and not the Druid or Keeper. She was a Fae with magic.

The thread gently pulled her toward the door. Twila allowed herself to be guided. Nyx chose to walk next to Twila, his big black glossy ears twitching. Scarlett and Trell followed closely behind. They walked out the door and Twila turned left, she had no idea where she was headed, but by the intake of breath behind her, she knew it was where they thought they would be heading. She didn't hurry, allowing the thread to guide her without urgency. They had made enough assumptions that had wasted time Twila would not rush this moment.

A few minutes and several more turns later found them at the top of a spiral staircase. "Is it telling you to go down the stairs?" Trell asked.

"Yes."

"I am going to insist on going first," Scarlett said.

"Why?" Twila asked, not bothered by the request, just curious.

"Because there is more down there than the Elven Ingress, and it's my responsibility."

Twila was not surprised by the mention of the Elven Ingress. After all, it's where she thought they were being led.

"What's down there?"

"The middle landing is the Gate to the land of Elves, the bottom is where the Forgotten Ones are kept."

Twila nodded her understanding. "And that's where you have Targon contained?"

"I have a bad feeling that he may not be as contained as he should be." Scarlett moved to the front. "Let me know if your magic says to go somewhere else." She took a step down the stairs, followed by Nyx, then Twila with Trell taking the final position.

"Do you honestly think Targon could escape a cell designed to hold the most powerful of the Enchanted Underworld?" Twila asked. "From what you both reported, he was an anxious delusional human with no magic."

"A few days ago, I would say no. But there was also no chance a human could enter Plane Three either, until Julian did."

"And that is the missing piece to the puzzle." Trell snapped his fingers, causing both women to turn their heads round to look up at him. "Targon is a Druid, which would allow him to enter The Keep."

"The Keep?" asked Scarlet.

"Before it was known as Area 52 or The Library, it was known as The Keep. Which is why you are known as The Keeper."

Twila was only half listening to them as the landing for the first floor came into view. The entrance to what she assumed was a room blazed with light. The thread in her hand went from a gentle pull to a more urgent tug. Scarlett moved off the stairs and halted in front of the entrance to a large room. Scarlett moved past her and into the room, allowing herself to be led. Tall statues of white marble towered over each side of the entrance with more inside the room. Absently, Twila noted the statues were Elven warriors holding open books, just like the others she had seen standing near places that held the keys to the gates. The thread did not immediately take her into the room but rather to the right statue and behind it where it made her kneel down as if dipping in place to tell her the crown had been here.

"What's it doing?" asked Scarlett.

"My best guess is telling me that Targon was roaming around longer than you thought and hid the crown here before going back up to the library to search for the Angel book."

"Well, he managed to open the Gate," Trell spoke.

Twila looked to where she had been avoiding. Her eyes had swept the room and taken in the shimmering wall at the opposite end of the room, the source of the brilliant light, but had chosen to continue to follow the magical thread in her hand.

"Nyx," Twila heard Scarlett command.

Without further words, the dog moved back to the stairs and bound down them. Twila moved to the center of the room, taking note of the book holding Elven warrior statues lining the wall. There were eight statues in total. Two near the stairs, two on each side of the room, and a final two at the entrance to the Gate. The two at the Gate were the first Twila had seen without books. They held swords aloft, blades crossed above the shimmering doorway. The doorway was massive and arched, glowing symbols etched on the outer rim, just like the images in the rooms that held the keys.

"Fuck," Scarlett swore loudly. "Nyx reports that cell three is open, and so is four and eight."

"Who are in four and eight?"

"Four is a Bear Shifter who attempted to assassinate the heads of all four Shifter Clans about seven years ago. He managed to kill two of them and three heirs."

"I remember," acknowledged Trell.

"And eight?" Twila asked, but returned her attention to the Gate.

Silence filled the room as she waited for an answer. Twila turned to face Scarlett who was looking at her with a blank expression.

"It's classified."

"I think we have passed the point of 'it's classified.' It may be relevant to what is happening now."

"Even if it is, I have to get clearance to tell you. Only two people know who is in that cell."

Twila had been in her position long enough to know there were times where being a Weapon still didn't give her authority enough to know everything. It was annoying but part of the job, and she had too much to think about with the Gate clearly accessed to worry about whoever was in cell eight.

"What are you planning to do?" Scarlett asked Twila.

"Follow the crown."

Twila looked at the large opening in wonder. Typically, the Portals into the other planes were invisible to the naked eye and you could see through them. The Gate, more commonly known as the Elven Ingress, opened onto a white floor with several stairs leading onto a vista that was completely unremarkable. No sound came through the Gate, giving it a more surreal feel. She looked at the weak sun high in the sky and then to Trell.

"Is it the same time on the other planes as where we enter from?"

He nodded. "Yes, and as the other planes are smaller in size, each one smaller than the next, when we travel, you won't cross timelines like you do on the human plane."

"Interesting," Twila commented. She looked around the room to make certain there was no one hiding. The room was empty aside from the large Elven statues. Using her magic, Twila continued to sense the Crown and the magical call it gave. It led directly into the Gate. She looked to Scarlett. "Can you please contact Katya and let her know I'm going to track the Crown?"

"Of course."

"Thanks." Twila closed her eyes and pictured herself in cream pants that would be serviceable in any weather, a white t-shirt, and a cream jacket with hood. Within seconds, she was now dressed in the image that had been in her head. Her black hair was wrapped around her head in two braids that wouldn't hinder her if she needed to fight.

Chapter 9
Twila

"Drop," Twila ordered.

She didn't wait to see if Trell complied, there was no time. A blade swished above her as she dropped to one knee and carried the momentum by rolling forward, further into the Elven Plane. Quickly Twila came to her feet and pulled out the two blades that were strapped across her back. She had created them before walking through the shimmering portal.

Blade struck blade and the clanging rang through the empty room. She held both her blades in front of her face, crossed, the attacker's blade halted in the center. It was a man with a salt and peppered shaggy black beard, gaunt-lined face, jet-black eyes, sallow-brown skin, and wide shoulders but with no bulk to him. He was much taller than her but looked like one good puff of wind would take him out. Her guess was it was the shifter Forgotten One from cell four.

They both took a step back and disengaged their blades. Twila looked over his shoulder to see Scarlett motioning to her. Lifting her two blades, she reversed them so the sharp edge now sat along her forearm.

"Why stop and attack?" Twila asked as she side-stepped another overhead swing. "Why not head deeper into the land of Elves?"

He didn't answer. Rather, he simply grunted and came at her with several quick strokes that she easily countered. He was slow and none of the blows were particularly strong nor precise. Her best guess was that he knew better than to try to use his powers to shift in the unstable environment.

"What did he offer you?" Twila continued to push.

Without hesitation, she ran at him, hitting him in the stomach with her shoulder and knocking him backwards. He lost his balance and stumbled. Seeing her chance, Twila, with precision and cold calculation, brought her blades up and one after the other in blindingly quick succession cut through sinew and bone to sever his hand from wrist. The Forgotten One screamed as the useless hand hit the hard floor, still clutching the hilt of his blade. The scream of pain turned into a roar of anger. He lost his mind and within the blink of an eye he transformed from man to bear. But something was wrong.

He was only part bear. The wild magic that had been released at the end of the Elven wars had obviously still not fully settled back into their leylines and was still unpredictable. Thankfully Twila had heeded Trell's warning and had created her blades and strengthened her wings, that were wrapped tightly around her bodice like a glowing white translucent waistcoat, while still in Area 52. The Shifter bellowed in what Twila guessed was agony as his body hovered between bear and man. The lower half of him was mostly bear, but patches of greying fur covered his torso, face, and arms.

In a calculated forced attack that was designed to keep him moving backward toward the gate, Twila ran at him, one sword held aloft at an angle over her head the other crossed over her body. She twirled the sword over her head and his eyes followed it as he took his first steps back toward the Elven Ingress and waiting witch.

With practiced ease, Twila stepped out with her right foot and twisted her body to bring her left leg up in a perfect round house kick. First her twirling blade sliced across his chest, causing him to hunch forward, before her left foot connected with his chin, propelling him through the gate and landing him on the flagstones at the feet of Scarlett.

Trell stood to the side of the gate open-mouthed. Twila smiled knowingly before turning her attention back to Scarlett. She watched the witch gesture to Nyx, who came to stand over the supine mess that was the half-transformed shifter. Twila waited. Her body tensed to leap back through the portal, if necessary. Scarlett seemed to have the escapee under control, but until he was bound, Twila would wait.

Trell came to stand beside her. "You ready?" he asked.

"Almost, just checking that Scarlett doesn't need our assistance."

They both watched as Scarlett waved her hands in the air before her, performing several intricate movements with her fingers. Her mouth moved, but of course no sound came through the barrier. The half-man, half-bear began to rise slowly off the floor. He had ceased moving, his arms now hung down. Scarlett had either rendered him unconscious or had made it impossible for him to move. The witch swung her arm in a wide gesture several times, like she was coiling something around him. Twila guessed that Scarlett had now bound him in some way.

Out of what seemed to be thin air, appeared four small, dark granite-colored creatures, as if just popping into existence. Twila looked on in wonder. It was not often she was surprised by the creatures of the Underworld, but these were the fabled gargoyles of the Court of Shadows. They had been put into the care of the then Keeper when the Elven Empire had fallen and had long been forgotten by many. The four gargoyles moved to the floating shifter and carefully held him. Scarlett flicked her wrist and the weight of the man had been transferred to the gargoyles. They carried him from the room.

Scarlett turned to the portal and waved to Twila and Trell. Twila gave her a thumbs up, which Scarlett returned.

"Now, we can go." She didn't wait to see how the lovers bid each other farewell, instead the Fae turned and looked out into the expanse of the Elven Plane.

They were standing in a small but grand pavilion—all white marble with veins of gold and full of shadows. Parts of the roof had crumbled and now rubble was scattered in places. One of the columns had a large crack down the center. The Elven Ingress Gate leading to the Keep was anchored between two large Elven statues, identical to the one on the other side.

Twila turned and walked to the top of the stairs. She looked out across the landscape. It felt stifled, forgotten, like gravestones in an abandoned cemetery where life in the outside world has moved forward. As far as the eye could see was bland, over-grown, but not destroyed. Dull, like the sun. Full of dirt, with patches of pale flowers or scratchy shrubs, if there was grass it was not a lush green, rather a faded beige.

"Where are we?"

"We are in the center of the Elven Plane. This is where each Court meets the other."

Carefully, she opened her magic, creating the barest open channel in the hope the Fae Crown could still be sensed. It was there but it felt different: the pull was clearer, the trail distinct. It was the opposite to what Twila had expected. She was cautiously optimistic.

"That way." She pointed to her right.

The sun was weak. Even though it was a clear sky there was hardly any warmth to the dull orange orb.

"Let's go." Trell said.

The two of them set out in silence. No wind whispering through trees, no birds overhead. Complete silence. It was a smidge unsettling.

The Druid cleared his throat politely. Twila looked over at him expectantly.

"Your fighting skills are impressive."

"Thank you." She didn't elaborate. What more could she say?

"Can I ask if you're using your magic to track the crown?"

"Yes, you can, and yes, I am. It's the finest channel I've ever done." Twila looked back out to the open landscape. The gentle but clear tug of the Fae Queen's crown continued to give off a satisfied hum that she was following correctly.

"Are you not worried about it backfiring like it did to the shifter? Both the magics you're using are internal forces," Trell asked, his concern clear in his voice.

Twila nodded. "I'm using a trickle of magic. He tried to transform his entire shape," she explained. "I understand the risk, but we really have little choice."

"Just don't push it. If it feels like something is changing, shut it down."

"But then we won't know where the crown is."

"True, but we also know that more than likely Targon is heading for the Sol Court to find the Angel's Scripture and that is our priority."

Twila considered what he said. While she would love to get her hands on the Fae Queen's crown, the need to claim the book that could teach anyone with enough power to open all the gates at once was vital to stopping Chaos. The crown had been used and the Elven Ingress Portal lay open—the book was their primary concern now.

"Do you know how to get to the Sol Court from here?" she asked.

"Yes, I've entered through the Elven Ingress before."

"The crown is pulling that way." She pointed diagonally to her right.

"Then it lines up at the moment."

They walked in silence, until they came to what was possibly once a paved road.

"Any suggestions?" Twila asked.

"We follow the road."

Twila noted the lack of vegetation near the road. "Aren't we out in the open a bit?"

Trell nodded. "Yes, we make ourselves seen, but then we also can't be ambushed."

"True, and with us not knowing who or what is out there, it's best to see what's coming at us," she reasoned. They moved onto the ancient road and continued to walk in the direction of the Sol Court.

"Can I ask you a question?" Twila asked as they stayed alert, their eyes sweeping the area, but her mind continued to process all the new information they had uncovered.

"Go ahead. We have several days' walk ahead of us."

"Why do you think you could sense Julian as a Druid but not Targon?" Twila asked.

"At this point, I'm not sure if he is a Druid, but it's the only explanation I can think of that allows him to not trigger anything in the Keep because he is human but also allows him to enter the Elven Plane without dying. When I met Julian, I was looking for something to answer that question. When I interrogated Targon, I wasn't aware he could enter another Plane so wasn't looking for it. I thought Druids were extinct, just the relic of me existing without reason."

The thin thread of magic Twila held gave a gentle tug to her right as the road they traveled veered left. She stopped.

"We have a problem."

"What?"

"The crown is going that way?" She nodded to the right.

Unexpectedly, this made Trell smile. "Good."

Twila watched him. "Care to tell me why?"

"That is the most direct route to the Sol Court," Trell explained.

"But?"

"But there is a large lake in the way. And my guess is there is not a boat or raft still watertight enough to get across it. Following the road will get us there quicker. He will have to follow the lake around and that will add time in the end." Trell smiled for a brief moment. "Finally, something is going our way."

Twila shook her head before continuing along the road. The thread of magic gave a slightly stronger pull as she walked in the other direction it wanted her to go.

"*You're going to have to trust me on this,*" she said through her magic. Twila tried to send a comforting thought through the connection but was careful not to use more of her magic. She had no wish to trigger anything in this ill begotten plane.

Chapter 10

Calliope

Calliope looked out the window. She felt the clunk of the landing gear and hatch settle into place as the plane sped through the crisp morning sky and barely refrained from tensing. *It's an hour and a half*, she chanted to herself as she closed her eyes against the pretty white clouds that sailed by and settled back into the plane seat. She needed something to distract her from the flight. Without opening her eyes, Calliope cleared her throat.

"Tell me how you feel about being a Druid," she said under her breath.

"Honestly, I feel weird," Julian answered just as quietly.

Calliope felt fingers gently pry her death grip on the arm rest away. Calliope cracked open her eye and watched Julian pat her hand reassuringly before placing it in her lap. Why was she suddenly disappointed that he hadn't tried to hold it?

"Weird, how?"

"Like I'm in limbo. I've had this huge title thrust upon me with no real indication that I have any powers other than I can enter a portal and come out in another plane. Trell claims my eidetic memory is a power. But there has been no chance for training or further explanations or guidance."

Calliope nodded. "That is all valid reasons for feeling weird. Wish I could help." And surprisingly, she actually meant it.

Before she could say more, they were interrupted by the cabin crew offering a snack and drink. Calliope ordered coffee and a muffin, while Julian took water and a cookie.

"Your turn," Julian said as he opened his bottle of water and took a sip.

"My turn what?" Calliope asked.

"Oh, come on, you know this is how we play. You ask a question; I ask a question."

Calliope rolled her eyes but didn't argue. "Fine, ask your question."

He lowered his head until his mouth was next to her ear, his hot breath sending a tingle down her spine. "Tell me why someone with wings is scared to fly?"

"Who said I'm scared to fly?"

Julian arched an eyebrow at her but didn't comment, nor did he move his face away.

"I think it's more of a control thing, than a scared thing," she finally admitted.

He kissed her cheek before she could pull away. "Now, that actually makes sense. Don't worry, Sunshine, I'll hold your hand on landing."

"Stop calling me that," she muttered, glaring at him.

He only laughed.

"It shouldn't be too much further," Calliope said as they followed a line of trees that Trell had told her how to find. To a passerby, they would have no meaning, but to a Druid, the brighter green-leafed tree spaced out amongst the darker ones native to the area showed a clear path. They had been following the tree guide for about half an hour. All the man-made trails had led away from where they were headed. The forest was almost a forgotten fixture of the area as the nearby Giant's Causeway garnered all the tourist attention.

"Wait," Calliope whispered, as she tugged on the sleeve of Julian's jacket. "Someone's here."

Julian nodded and slowed, allowing her to move forward. Calliope liked the way he deferred to her

with no show of ego. For a brief moment, she wondered if Apollo would do the same. Possibly not.
After all, a Wyvern Lord didn't get to his position by
deferring to anyone.

Several twigs cracked and there was a loud sneeze
that echoed through the forest. Whoever was there
was making no effort to hide themselves. Calliope
frowned but kept moving toward the sound. She
stopped when she came to the edge of the clearing.

Two massive elm trees with wide gnarled trunks
stood to the back of an altar. Their branches were
large enough that they created a thick canopy that
covered the entire moss covered clearing. Between
those trunks was the portal known as the Troll's
Doorway. The large altar was made of black marble
and rose quartz. But what made Calliope halt was
the creature that was doubled over studying a glowing glyph on the front of the altar.

"It's about time you got here," the troll said as he
straightened.

"You knew we were coming?" Calliope asked cautiously as she stepped into the clearing.

"Yes, but we can get to that in a moment." He
pointed to a glowing shape on the altar. "What I
want to know is who entered the Elven Plane and
triggered this?"

Chapter 11

Katya

"Kat, I need you to pull rank and get to the Queen now. She needs to meet me in the sigil room." Scarlett didn't bother with any greeting which put Katya on alert immediately.

"Has something happened to Twila?" Katya interrupted.

Scarlett shook her head vigorously. "No, she's fine. But that's all I can say at the moment."

"Okay," Katya said. She was used to following orders without always knowing the whole thing, but this was highly unusual coming from the Keeper. She could almost sense the urgency through the fake phone she used to communicate with Scarlett on the human realm.

Scarlett went on. "I dare not leave for more than a few moments, but this message must be delivered in person. There must be no one else in the room."

Kat nodded.

"You also need to be clear that she needs to double her guard and Jaz is possibly a target." Scarlett's face contorted into a grimace. "I wish I could tell you more."

Kat nodded as she tried to take in all the instructions without jumping to conclusions. The mention of Jaz made her feel slightly ill. Kat had only heard from Jaz not fifteen minutes ago confirming that they had arrived at the portal and were about to enter.

"I'll arrive in half an hour."

"That's not a lot of time."

"There's no time for pomp and ceremony. The Queen has wings and power, it's time to use them," Scarlett said in her usual direct tone.

Kat blinked at that. "I'll see you in half an hour," she assured Scarlett.

Quickly she closed the phone and shoved it into her pocket. On instinct, Kat removed the court dress she had put on this morning and created black cargo pants and an amber-colored vest. She brought her wings in and wrapped them around her torso, creating a shiny tough armor, and finished the look with black combat boots. Kat walked out of the bedroom and into the small sitting room, heading toward the desk she worked at when her paperwork was due. With practiced ease, she strapped the black leather belt that held two knives around her waist and carefully placed another two shorter throwing blades into the pile of dark curls she had pulled up into a messy bun.

"Kat?" a voice called. It was Dryadon. He came from the bathroom.

"I don't have time to explain. You have to go back on your own."

"No, no, that's not it."

She looked expectantly at the handsome dark-skinned Oracle, but didn't stop moving. She bent and tucked a final blade into the side of her boot. He didn't look surprised at her change of clothing or collection of weapons that now adorned her.

"Trust no one," he said softly.

"What?" she asked as she straightened.

His brown eyes were earnest and trying to convey something. "Much will be revealed, but even those you trust most are keeping their own council."

Katya moved to him, watching him. "Even you?"

"Never, but I can only give you what is given to me to interpret. And at the moment I see echoes of the past, wrapped in dark wings and things whispered in corners, but the light is creeping in."

"You talk in riddles." She shook her head. "I have to go." She fought the urge to reach out and touch his cheek. That would be too much affection shown and that was not something she would ever do.

Trust no one, echoed in her head. His words had shaken her, but she held it in check. Kat needed to deal with Scarlett's urgent request first.

Without saying goodbye, she hurried from the room and ran down the corridor, startling the guards posted at either end of the hallway. She sprinted down the stairs and continued to run as she left the residence section and entered the official part of the palace where she hoped the Queen would be in her office, taking care of her morning meetings. Kat arrived at the door and spoke with a firmness she rarely employed.

"I need to speak to the Queen, now."

One guard looked to the door and then back again, while the other bristled at her words but gave a nod.

"Wait," he ordered.

Katya held her words in check as she watched him politely tap on the door. The Queen's Seneschal opened the door and looked expectantly at the guard.

"Katya requires an immediate audience with the Queen," he said quietly. Katya could hear the disdain for the lack of protocol she had used.

The Seneschal looked over to Katya and waited. Katya gave her a tight grimace.

"I wouldn't do this without reason."

The older Fae tilted her head to the side for a moment before nodding. "Very well, come in."

Both guards moved a step to the side to allow her through. Katya found Stellamaris sitting at her desk, nectar cup in hand, reading a large book. Katya moved quickly to the desk and bowed.

"I'm sorry to intrude but there was no time. I've been contacted by the Keeper who has insisted upon an odd request."

"Seneschal Fenera, please find me General Owen or Captain Kirkpatrick."

The older Fae bowed. "Yes, Your Majesty."

She hurried from the room.

They were now alone.

"Speak freely," Stellamaris ordered.

She put the crystal cup down, giving Katya her undivided attention.

"Scarlett has asked for you to meet her at the sigil room. There is to be no one there. She said she could not leave Area 52 for very long but that whatever she had to say she needed to say in person."

The Fae Queen closed the book and stood, unfurling her wings as she did.

"Anything else?"

"She told me to double your guard and that Jaz might be in more danger than we thought."

"When does she want to meet?"

"You have twenty minutes to get there."

"I don't know if that is possible. Guards will need to be assembled, people told that I'm leaving."

Katya shook her head. "She was explicit that it had to be now. Her words were. 'She has wings and power and it's time she used them.'"

Stellamaris' blonde eyebrows raised but she didn't comment. A knock on the door interrupted any further conversation. Captain Kirkpatrick opened the door without waiting for an answer. He didn't look surprised to see his squad leader standing there so Kat assumed Seneschal Fenera had told him she had been the messenger.

"Your Majesty sent for me?" he said as soon as the door was closed.

"Yes, the Keeper needs to see me and has sent a warning that Jaz may be in danger and to double my guards."

Kirkpatrick didn't miss a beat. "We can do that."

"The Keeper has asked me to meet her in the sigil room, by myself, in approximately fifteen minutes," Stellamaris told him.

He turned to Katya. "Anything else?"

Kat hesitated for a second, but in the end, her loyalty and trust of the two people in the room won.

"Dryadon also warned me to trust no one and that people close to me are keeping their own secrets."

"And yet you're telling us?" Kirkpatrick looked at her.

She shrugged. "If I can't trust you two then what's the point of being a Weapon?"

"Good. Let's do this without fuss. I'm going to rush out of here and bellow for General Owen. While I do that, you two are going to slip out the window and fly directly to the sigil room." He looked to Kat. "You come and go often enough that everyone should recognize you to get you into the tower." He turned to the Queen. "When you get there, dress like Katya. Nothing that says 'I'm the Queen.' People expect you to look a certain way, so it should give you enough cover for Kat to get you up to the room and then it's up to you both on how you clear the room for the meeting."

Kirkpatrick walked to the window and threw it open saying loudly. "It's stuffy in here, Your Majesty, a little breeze may help." He turned back to the two Fae. "Have your meeting but don't leave the tower. Owen or I will be there with your guards to escort you back."

It didn't take long for Katya and Queen Stella-maris to shift into their natural tiny form and fly out the open window, leaving Kirkpatrick to keep the palace focused on his demands to find General Owen. Katya led the way, thankful the Crystal Palace sat adjacent to grounds of the temple where the tower sat with its room of sigils at the top. She tried to do the math and knew they would be cutting it close.

Approximately ten minutes later, they halted at the guarded door of the square, squat tower. It got its name for being the highest building in the Fae Realm of the Enchanted Underworld, standing on the highest hill, overlooking the city. Not for its grand appearance, for it was truly nondescript in all the ways that were important.

Katya began to spin slowly on the spot, transforming into her human shape and returning to the clothes she had worn prior. Kat stopped spinning and landed gently on the cobbled path and waved in a friendly greeting as she walked to the door.

"Hey, sorry for the zero notice but something came up. I know I've got clearance but my newbie doesn't. Is that going to be a problem?"

"If you vouch for her, that's good enough. We'll just have to note her name for the records."

Kat turned to the sound of boots on the cobblestones. She kept the shock of seeing the Queen attired as a Weapon from her face as she nodded her approval. Stellamaris had indeed taken Kirkpatrick's suggestion to dress the same as Katya literally, though it was in the colors of her own wings. While Katya wore black pants and boots, the Queen wore crisp white and her vest was the softest of blues that glowed with the sheen of her gossamer wings wrapped around her torso. The Fae Queen was slender and looked more angular with the tighter clothing and her strawberry blonde hair pulled back in a single braid down her back.

"They just need your name," Kat told her.

"Ella." Stellamaris smiled as she answered.

One of the guards took her name, while the other returned the smile.

"Wish we could chat, but you know how it is," Katya joked as she pushed open the door and held it open for 'Ella.'

They hurried in to find more guards and other people going about their business. Some were waiting for approval to travel, or their time to arrive. Kat nodded to several people but didn't stop to talk as she headed for the stairs.

"Ella, we're running late. I'm going to run. Follow as quickly as you can."

"Go, go," Ella said quietly. "I should be safe enough here. I won't be that far behind you."

Kat didn't wait. She took the stairs two at a time, excusing herself as she hurried past several people on their way up or down the stairs. Three floors later and she stood at the door to the sigils.

"Shit," she muttered as she took in the scene of a room packed with people. How was she supposed to get them all out without raising suspicion or gossip?

"Fire!" she yelled loudly into the noisy room. Katya grabbed the closest guard. "Get everyone out. There's a fire in a room on the second floor."

"But... I don't smell anything." He hesitated.

"And?" a voice asked behind him. He turned to find Ella there, hands on her hips. Small but oozing authority. "Get these people out now, or would you like to answer to General Owen when asked why you didn't follow orders?"

"Fire," Kat yelled again, moving deeper into the room. Half the people began to move towards the door, while the other half asked what was happening. Both Kat and Ella moved around the room, assuring people that they were safe and the fire was contained but that they needed to head to ground floor until the all clear was given.

The room was cleared in a short time, and as Kat closed the door, a loud deep gong echoed once around the room. They had done it.

Queen Stellamaris walked over to a small alcove that was covered by a tall urn with a long-stalked plant obscuring the view behind it. The sigil that operated the portal to Area 52 was hidden in plain sight. Everyone knew about the seven that move you through the provinces of the Enchanted Underworld but not the one hidden in the tiny space behind the plant.

"Move aside," Scarlett said from the other side of the plant.

Kat and Stellamaris did what they were told. The urn moved slowly forward, allowing Scarlett to step around it. She curtsied quickly.

"Your Majesty. Thank you for coming."

"I understand you don't have a lot of time. Don't stand on ceremony. Just tell me what I need to know."

"Targon, the thief who tried to steal The Keeper's Tome is probably a Druid," the witch began. "Twila believes that he brought the Fae Crown with him and hid it before going in search of the book. He managed to get himself out of the cell and freed two prisoners before opening the Elven Ingress and entering. The portal is now open and Twila and Trell have gone through." Scarlett looked quickly at Kat and then back to the Queen. "We already have one prisoner back in custody. Prisoner four."

Queen Stellamaris nodded. "None of this requires me here. What aren't you saying?"

"The other prisoner to escape was number eight." Again Kat noticed Scarlett quickly look at her and then away.

"Who's prisoner eight?" Katya asked.

The Keeper looked to the Fae Queen. "Tell her."

"Your father."

Chapter 12

Jazlynn

Jazlynn broke off contact with Katya but didn't close her mind fully as she nodded for everyone to move out.

"Ready?" Cael asked her from behind, his hand taking hers and squeezing it gently.

"Yes," she said softly, while returning with a quick squeeze of her own. A thought occurred to her as she walked toward the portal, following the guards in front. "Do you know what Court it opens into?" she asked, turning her head slightly.

"From what I could see, it was the Court of Shadows."

Jaz nodded to show she had heard what he'd said as she stood before the portal. Taking a breath and keeping only the slightest of channels open, she walked through the portal and into the Elven Plane.

"Welcome, Princess," a cold, hard voice greeted her. "Don't do anything stupid or your men die."

The first five guards that had been sent through were kneeling in front of a robed figure. Standing on either side of the dark robed man, stood a pale-faced creature taller than any being she had ever met—a female troll with weathered ash colored skin, a flat nose, and protruding chin. On the other side stood a male Vila, with deep-brown toned skin and glittery green eyes. They both wore shimmery grey robes with a deep cowl that only showed their faces. Several more creatures from the Enchanted Underworld stood in a larger semicircle. They had arrows notched and ready to fire.

Jazlynn took it all in with one glance, and several things fell into place at once. She now understood how the enemies were traveling easily through the realms without using the portals. She halted just past the portal, allowing the person behind her to come through. Cael. He came to stand beside her, his face telling her everything she needed to know.

"You knew."

"I'm sorry," he said quietly. "Just cooperate and it will be over soon."

Jazlynn turned as if to face him but continued her turn until she was facing the portal. The next guard walked through and she took action immediately.

She shoved him back through and as she did, she told him, "Warn them."

He stumbled backwards and fell back through the portal.

"Aren't you a clever one," the cold voice commented. "No more of that Princess, or I start killing your guards."

Jaz turned back and faced the black robed figure. She lifted her head defiantly.

"Cuff her," he ordered.

The Vila in his grey robes moved toward her with a pair of cuffs that looked suspiciously similar to the ones she had put on Cael's wrists not that long ago to dampen his magic. The grey robes pulled at her memories, and she racked her brain to figure out what.

"Hold out your hands. Wrists together," Cael told her. She didn't look at him as she did what she was told. Jaz was too focused on the grey shimmering robe of the Vila.

It came to her in a rush and Jaz threw her mind's voice far and wide, hoping that someone would hear her as the Vila reached her. *They're using the Ghosts Avenue to...* The cool metal bracelets snapped closed and an odd numbing sensation spread throughout her body.

Jaz's world went silent.

Continue the Journey Here:
Elven Ingress: Gates of Ascension, Book 2

A captive princess. A family divided.
An ancient gateway opened.

The Elven Ingress lies open.
Half-truths have surfaced. Deeper secrets remain
buried. And the Weapons of the Fae Queen are
forced to question everything they thought they
knew.
Not just about their enemy.
But about love.
And blood.
Because when legacy and loyalty collide, even the
strongest bonds can fracture.
And once a gate is opened...
Nothing—and no one—remains untouched.

A steamy paranormal romance of love, family, and
secrets powerful enough to change the fate of the
realms.

Acknowledgments

I would like to take a few moments
to say thank you.

To my children, thank you for
teaching me to let go of the small stuff. I am proud
of you.

To my family, thank you for the
love and support you have shown me throughout
the years.

To my friends, the ones that have
my back and are forever in my corner – I cherish
you.

To my ARC, Street, Beta, and Proofreader Teams.
You are appreciated.

About Taya Rune

Taya Rune is a writer of romance, a sucker for happy endings, and has a knack for asking people uncomfortable questions.

She is a USA Today Bestselling Author and a finalist for the 2022 Romantic Book of the Year, for the Romance Writer's of Australia RuBY awards.

She has had her work published in many anthologies and publications.

Taya also writes under the pen names Everly Bane (MM/BL Romance), M.M. Reynolds (Epic Fantasy), and A.J Belle (Children's Books).

To receive up-to-date information, news and
exclusive offers online please sign up
for the Taya Rune newsletter.

www.tayarune/subscribe.com

Follow her on your favorite platform:

Website:
https://www.tayarune.com

Facebook
https://www.facebook.com/taya.rune.75

Facebook Group
https://www.facebook.com/groups/tayasromanti
crealm

TikTok
https://www.tiktok.com/@tayarune

Instagram
https://www.instagram.com/tayarune/

Bookbub
https://www.bookbub.com/authors/taya-rune

Goodreads
https://www.goodreads.com/author/show/21156
065.Taya_Rune

Taya Rune